How to... Series

How to BABYSIT YOUR GROWN-UP

Activities to Do Together

Jean Reagan WITH JaNay Brown-Wood   ILLUSTRATED BY Lee Wildish

Alfred A. Knopf
New York

To JaNay, Lee, and the whole PRH
team for their expertise, and to
Sandra for her wise laughter

—J.R.

THIS IS A BORZOI BOOK PUBLISHED BY ALFRED A. KNOPF

Text copyright © 2023 by Jean Reagan
Text by Jean Reagan and JaNay Brown-Wood
Cover art and interior illustrations copyright © 2023 by Lee Wildish

Visit us on the Web! rhcbooks.com

Educators and librarians, for a variety of teaching tools, visit us at RHTeachersLibrarians.com

Library of Congress Cataloging-in-Publication Data is available upon request.
ISBN 978-0-593-47923-0 (trade) — ISBN 978-0-593-56890-3 (lib. bdg.) — ISBN 978-0-593-47924-7 (ebook)

The text of this book is set in 16-point Goudy Old Style MT Pro.
The illustrations were created digitally.
Interior design by Monique Razzouk

MANUFACTURED IN CHINA
10 9 8 7 6 5 4 3 2 1

First Edition

Contents

FUN . . . WITH CRAFTS

FUN . . . WITH IMAGIN-YAY-TION

FUN . . . WITH FAMILY

CHECKLIST

Introduction

Ready to keep your grown-up busy? AND to have lots of fun? Great!

In this book, you'll find all kinds of things to do, create, and learn—*together!* All you need are basic materials and a little imagination. Some of the activities will need an adult's help.

Ready, set, GO!

FUN . . .
in the Fresh Air

How to Make an Easy-Peasy Kite

SUPPLIES YOU'LL NEED:

A plastic grocery bag
Two very long pieces of string or yarn

STEPS:

Uh-oh, did I miss a spot?

1. Peek out the window. Is it sunny? YAY!
2. Put on your summer clothes—quick!
3. Slather on some sunblock.
4. Tie one piece of string onto one handle of the plastic grocery bag. Then tie the second piece of string onto the second handle. Make sure each knot is nice and tight.
5. Hold the two pieces of string in your hand.
6. Head outside and run full speed, with the kite catching the wind behind you. How high does it go?

How to Plant a Seed

SUPPLIES YOU'LL NEED:

An apple
A disposable cup and spoon
Soil
A window that gets some sunshine
Water

STEPS:

1. Eat one tasty apple until only the core is left. Pull one seed from the core and set it aside.
2. Use the spoon to fill the cup with soil.
3. Gently make a hole in the center of the soil as deep as the tip of your finger. Place your apple seed in the hole and cover it with soil.
4. Drop a little bit of water onto the soil. Place the cup near a sunny window.
5. Water the seed a little bit every three days. Watch it grow, and grow, and grow!
6. Once the plant gets big enough, find a sunny spot in the yard for the baby tree! With a grown-up, dig a small hole.
7. Use a spoon to lift the soil and plant out of the cup. Place the plant and soil into the hole. Add a little more soil and pat it.
8. Water your little plant each week and watch it grow.

Ideas of other seeds to plant:

- ☆ Sweet pea
- ☆ Bell pepper
- ☆ Sunflower
- ☆ Cucumber

How to Make a Leaf Collector's Book

SUPPLIES YOU'LL NEED:

A small bag
Leaves
A library book about leaves
Tape
Sheets of paper
A stapler

Maple

Linden

STEPS:

1. Go for a walk with a grown-up and take along a small bag.
2. Keep an eye out for cool-looking leaves. Add your favorites to your bag until it's full.
3. Back at home, spread out your leaves.
4. Pick one leaf to start. Look closely. Does it have one pointy tip or more? Is it flat and fat or thin with spiky needles poking out?
5. Stack leaves that look alike until you have a few piles.

6. Flip through your library book, or find a leaf identification website and look for a leaf that matches.

7. Tape the leaf to a piece of paper and write the leaf's name under it. Continue doing this with your other leaves.

8. Staple the pages together.

9. Next time you go on a walk, take your new leaf book. Spot and name the leaves that you see.

Elm

Tulip Poplar

Quaking Aspen

Other nature books you can make:

- ★ A rock book with drawings identifying rocks
- ★ A flower book with flowers from around your home and community
- ★ A bug book with drawings of bugs you see

How to Camp in Your Backyard

SUPPLIES YOU'LL NEED:

Paper and a pencil
A tote bag—the biggest you can find
Two blankets
Snacks
Four chairs
Four large stuffed animals

Is she here now?

STEPS:

1. Make a list of snacks you'll need for tonight.
2. Wait for Grandma to get to your house.
3. When she arrives, hurry her to your room.
4. Hand Grandma two rolled-up blankets to stuff inside the tote bag.
5. Give her your snack list and a thumbs-up. As she gathers the treats, carefully carry four chairs and the tote bag to the backyard.
6. Lay out one blanket on the grass and set a chair at each corner of the blanket.

7. Take the other blanket out and drape it over the chairs.
8. Hurry back inside and grab four of your largest stuffed animals. Set them in the chairs so they hold the blanket in place.
9. Make space for Grandma—and the snacks.
10. Tell stories in your tent and watch the sunset.

How to Make a Snowman

SUPPLIES YOU'LL NEED:

Lots and lots of snow
Warm clothes
Two pencils or empty paper towel rolls
Two buttons
A carrot
A piece of yarn
A fuzzy hat

There. Because snowmen get cold, too!

FREE COOKIES

STEPS:

1. Wait for snow! When there are a few inches on the ground, bundle up in your warmest clothes. Make sure your grown-ups have their warm clothes on, too—they get cold really easily.
2. Show your grown-ups how to pack snow into a large snowball.
3. Then roll it on the ground, gathering more snow to make it bigger and bigger. Together, repeat this with a medium-sized snowball and a small one.
4. Make sure the biggest snowball is on the bottom. Flatten its top and then put the second-biggest snowball over it. Pat that one, too, and add the smallest ball—that's the head!
5. Poke the pencils or paper towel rolls in the side of the second snowball for arms. Then place the two buttons in the top snowball as eyes, the carrot as a nose, and the piece of yarn as a smile.
6. Something's missing! Oh yes! Place your fuzzy hat on top of the snowman's head.

How to Enjoy a Picnic

SUPPLIES YOU'LL NEED:

A basket
Tasty snacks
A blanket

STEPS:

1. Chat with your parents about which nearby parks have big, green spaces. Pick the perfect one.
2. Fill your basket with snacks like applesauce cups, cheese sticks, animal crackers, bananas, and granola bars—or anything tasty you have in your kitchen!
3. Check the linen closet for a blanket. Head to the park with your family.
4. Find a nice open space, put down your basket, and lay out the blanket.
5. If Mom's busy with the baby, help her with the snacks.
6. Share your favorite jokes under the bright blue sky.

Other ideas of where to have a picnic:

⭐ On the front lawn or in the backyard
⭐ At the beach
⭐ On your patio
⭐ In the back of a truck
⭐ In your living room on a rainy day

How to Go Stargazing

SUPPLIES YOU'LL NEED:

A flashlight

STEPS:

1. Wait for nighttime—this won't work if it isn't dark.
2. Lead your grown-up out into the yard. Bring a flashlight, too, in case they feel a little scared.
3. Look up. Use your imagination to connect the star-dots to make a shape. Point it out to your grown-up.
4. Ask your grown-up what they know about stars. Listen closely—you may learn something new!
5. Try to count the stars in the sky. As you count, do you notice anything moving up there from the side of your eye? Maybe it's a shooting star! Close your eyes and make a wish.
6. Kiss your grown-up on the cheek and say, "I love you to the stars and back!"

FUN . . .
with Paper

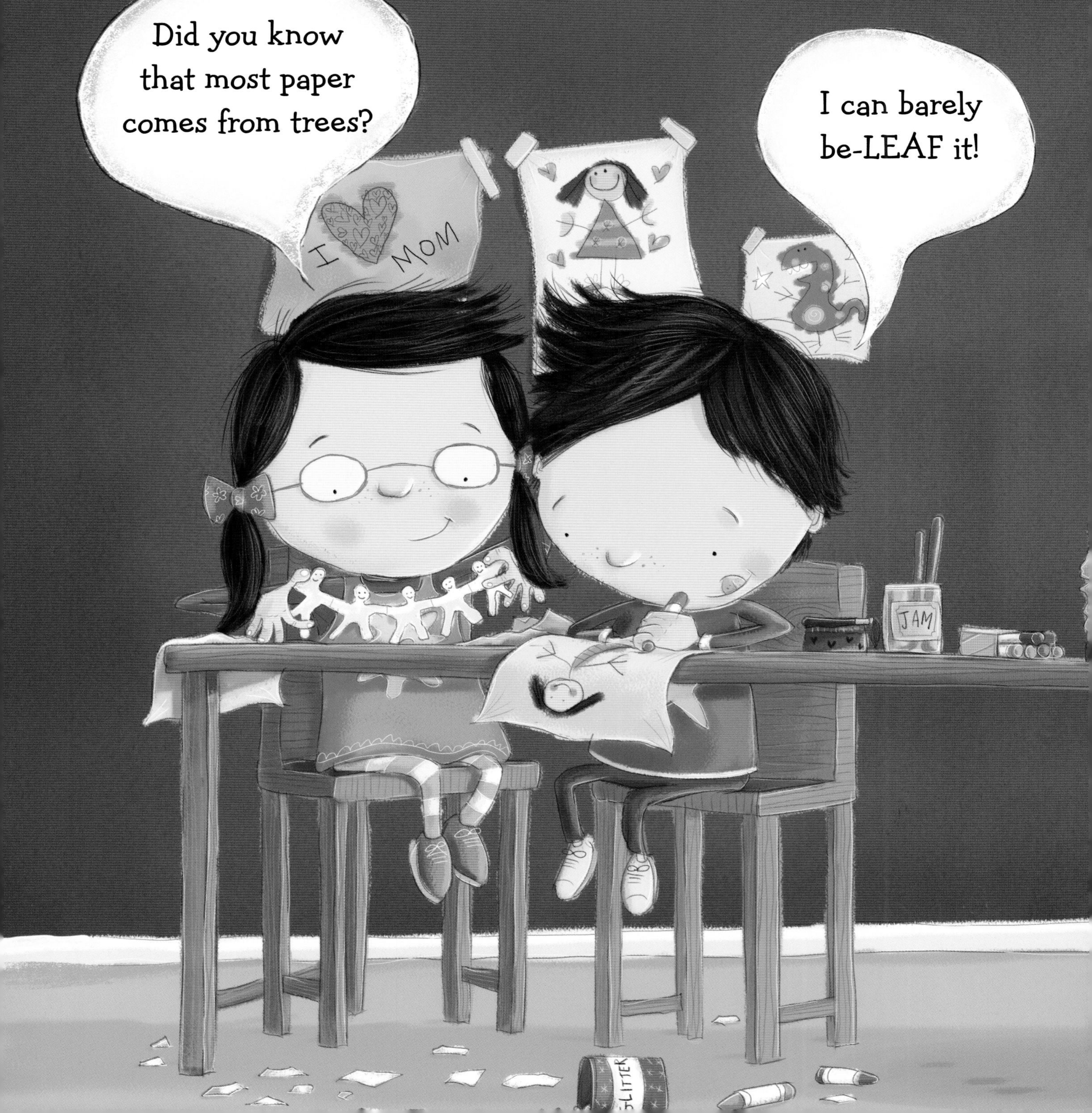

How to Make a Mosaic

SUPPLIES YOU'LL NEED:

A large piece of paper

Different-colored construction paper, tissue
  paper, or pages from an old magazine

A glue stick

STEPS:

1. Use your imagination to draw a cool scene on the large piece of paper.
2. Rip the colorful construction paper, tissue paper, or old magazine pages into very small pieces—like the size of a dime or quarter. Make piles of different colors.
3. With a glue stick, add glue to your drawing. Stick on different colors of ripped paper to complete the scene.
4. Watch your mosaic take shape!

Ideas of what to create for your mosaic:

☆ Animals in a jungle
☆ Fish under the sea
☆ Your favorite trucks
☆ Shapes of different sizes

How to Make a Snowflake

SUPPLIES YOU'LL NEED:

A square piece of paper
Kid-safe scissors
Glue
Glitter
String (optional)

STEPS:

1. Fold your square of paper diagonally in half, from one corner across to another, so it becomes a big triangle.

2. Fold it again in half, joining the two far corners, so that you make another, smaller triangle. Repeat two more times. Now you should have a small folded triangle.

3. With a grown-up's help, use your scissors to cut off the ends at the bottom of your triangle, as in the picture. Try cutting small and large triangles along each edge of the paper. You can even snip off the points of the triangles—but be careful not to cut all the way across the triangle or else it might not work.

4. Unfold the triangle. Surprise!
5. If you like, spread glue on your snowflake and sprinkle on some glitter. Set aside to dry.
6. Cut a small hole at the top of the snowflake and tie a piece of string through the hole.
7. Have your grown-up hang it up for everyone to see!

How to Send a Letter to Grandpa

SUPPLIES YOU'LL NEED:

A sheet of paper
Your favorite markers
An envelope
A stamp

STEPS:

1. Create a secret message to your grandpa using your markers. Draw a picture or write words!

2. Fold the paper to hide the message.

3. Slip it into the envelope. Seal it tightly!

4. With a grown-up's help, write Grandpa's name and address on the front of the envelope in the center. In the top left corner, write your name and address.

5. Peel the paper off the back of the stamp and stick it in the top right corner of your envelope.

6. Put your envelope into a mailbox at the post office or in the community, or in your own mailbox so your mail carrier will see it.

SAM
MY STREET
MY ROAD

To Grandpa.
Grandpa's house
Grandpa's street.

Other people to send letters to:

☆ Your best friend
☆ Your teacher
☆ A pen pal
☆ Santa Claus
☆ Yourself!

How to Make
Your Own Book

SUPPLIES YOU'LL NEED:

A large sheet of paper
Kid-safe scissors

STEPS:

1. Turn the large sheet of paper on its side so the long side is closest to you.
2. Fold the sheet hot-dog-style by pulling the top of the sheet down and lining it up with the bottom.
3. Now, take the folded sheet and fold it again, this time in half from one side to the other, hamburger-style. Repeat this once more.
4. Unfold the paper all the way. It will have lots of creases that make rectangles. Fold it hamburger-style again, just once.

5. With your grown-up's help, use your scissors to cut a line along the middle crease, from the edge that is folded to the center. Stop in the middle! See the picture for help.

6. Unfold your whole sheet once more and find the slit right in the middle. Fold the sheet in half again, from top to bottom, hot-dog-style.

7. Grab opposite sides of the folded paper and push them toward the center until you see the slit open into the shape of a diamond. Keep pushing until the diamond gets very skinny and becomes a slit again.

8. Fold the paper so the rectangles are all on top of each other. It doesn't matter which way you start this fold. Now, it should look like a tiny book. Run your finger over all the creases again so they are very sharp.

Ideas of what to put in your book:

✫ Drawings of your family or friends
✫ Your favorite words
✫ A story
✫ Funny jokes

9. Fill the pages of your book with stories, pictures, or anything you'd like. On the front cover, write your title and your name!

How to Make Your Own Puzzle

SUPPLIES YOU'LL NEED:

Card stock or light cardboard (such as from a cereal box)
Markers, paint, or crayons
A ruler or something straight
A pencil
Kid-safe scissors

STEPS:

1. Make sure your card stock or cardboard is in the shape of a rectangle.
2. Use markers, paint, or crayons to decorate the rectangle with your artwork.

3. Flip the artwork over. Put your ruler in the middle of your rectangle, going hot-dog-style. With a pencil, make a line across the length. Use the pencil to lightly make a line on the back of the puzzle.

4. Next, use your ruler and ask your grown-up to help you make three marks each on the top and bottom edges of the puzzle so that you can make four equal-sized strips. Use the ruler and the pencil to connect the top and bottom dots to make those lines.

5. With the help of your grown-up, cut along the light pencil lines so you have eight rectangles.

6. Mix the rectangles up and then solve your puzzle. Have a grown-up try next.

Ideas for different puzzle shapes:

☆ Different-sized triangles
☆ Random shapes
☆ Skinny rectangular strips
☆ Squiggly-shaped pieces

How to Make and Play Animal Card Memory

SUPPLIES YOU'LL NEED:

Two pieces of paper or card stock
Markers
Kid-safe scissors

STEPS:

1. Fold one piece of paper or card stock in half, side to side, hamburger-style, twice. Then fold it in half, top to bottom, once.

2. Unfold the card stock so you can see the creases. Cut at the creases. Repeat all of these steps for the second piece of paper or card stock. You now have sixteen rectangles.

3. Draw a picture of a different animal on each of the eight rectangles. On each of the remaining rectangles, write the name of one of the animals. For example, if you drew a dog on one rectangle, you should have "dog" written on another.

4. Now you are ready to play Animal Card Memory! Mix up the cards and lay them facedown.

5. Each turn, someone flips over two cards searching for matches. If they find a match, they act out the animal's sounds and movements to keep the cards. They then get to go again.

6. If they flip over two cards that are not a match, they turn the cards back over in the same spot. Next person's turn!

7. The game is over when all the matches are found.

How to Make Super-Spy Ink

SUPPLIES YOU'LL NEED:

One lemon
Water
A bowl
Q-tips
Some white printer paper
An envelope

STEPS:

1. Ask your grown-up to cut the lemon in half. Squeeze lemon juice into a small bowl. Drop in about five drops of water using your fingertips and then use a Q-tip to stir the mix.
2. Make sure the Q-tip is very wet with the juice.
3. On a practice piece of paper, write out a fun code—this part is just to make sure it works. Dip the Q-tip back into the juice as needed to write your code. Set aside to dry completely.
4. Once the juice message is dry, hold the paper close to a lamp. Watch the message magically appear! Perfect!
5. Now pull out a new sheet of paper and write out a super-secret message to Grandpa. On an envelope, write "For Grandpa's Eyes Only."
6. When your message is dry, put it into the envelope. Seal it shut.
7. Deliver it to Grandpa and whisper, "Hold it near a light for a secret message."
8. Mission accomplished!

How to Build a Volcano

SUPPLIES YOU'LL NEED:

Modeling clay or Play-Doh
Goggles or sunglasses
Plastic spoons
Baking soda
Vinegar
A small measuring cup with spout
Food coloring (optional)

STEPS:

1. First, make a small volcano using modeling clay or Play-Doh. Make a deep hole for the ingredients. Set it aside to dry.

2. Put on the goggles. Sunglasses work just fine, too!

3. Scoop out about two tablespoons of baking soda. Dump it into your volcano.

4. Pour some vinegar into the measuring cup. Add food coloring and stir. Red makes for GREAT lava!

It's gonna blow!!!

5. Carefully pour a little colored vinegar into the hole—slowly, slowly, slowly.

6. Stand back and watch the science in action! So cool!

7. Wipe out the volcano and repeat!

Other materials for building your volcano:

⭐ Dirt or sand. Same effect as using clay?

⭐ Bread molded into a volcano shape and then dried. Did that work?

⭐ Glued cotton balls. Any luck?

How to Make a Lava Lamp

SUPPLIES YOU'LL NEED:

Hippie clothes and a big wig (optional)

An empty jar and lid

Water

Food coloring

Glitter (optional)

Cooking oil

Alka-Seltzer tablets (with an
adult's help—kids
shouldn't handle
medicine!)

STEPS:

1. Look through your dress-up clothes for hippie clothes and a big wig—the bigger, the better. If you don't have one, find other ways to dress like a groovy hippie.

2. In the kitchen, fill the jar less than halfway with water.

3. Drop some food coloring into the jar. Sprinkle in some glitter if using it.

4. Carefully pour in the cooking oil so it almost fills the jar. Be sure to leave some space at the very top.

5. Ask your grown-up to break the Alka-Seltzer into pieces and drop them in, one at a time. Watch the gas make the bubbles dance!

6. Now put a lid on your jar. Shake it while you hold it up to a light. Instant lava lamp!

Questions to explore: How did that happen?

☆ Make a hypothesis (known as an educated guess) about why that happened.

☆ Go to a computer and search "What happens when you mix oil and water?" Did you guess correctly?

How to Make Goop

SUPPLIES YOU'LL NEED:

A large bowl

Two cups cornstarch

One cup water

A large spoon

Food coloring (optional)

Small bowls or sandwich-sized plastic zip bags (optional)

Small washable figurines, buttons, or other toys (optional)

Paper towels

STEPS:

1. Dump cornstarch into the large bowl. As you slowly pour in the water, mix with the spoon. Continue pouring and mixing until it's the consistency you want.

2. Add in food coloring as desired. If you want many different colors, scoop some of the Goop into separate bowls or sandwich-sized zip bags and then add different-colored drops to each.

3. You can explore the Goop with your hands or play around with spoons, small plastic figurines, buttons—anything washable. Keep your paper towels nearby to wipe your hands. If your Goop is in a bag, seal it and squish away.

Questions to explore: How did that happen?

★ Think about why the cornstarch and water reacted the way they did.

★ Go to the library and look for a book with science experiments.

★ See if you can find the answer about how those ingredients made that cool Goop—also called Oobleck.

★ If you can't find a book, ask your adult to look online with you to find the answer.

How to Watch a Vegetable Drink

SUPPLIES YOU'LL NEED:

Paper cups
Water
Food coloring
Celery stalks with leaves still attached
A small tray or takeout container top
A marker

STEPS:

1. Fill the cups less than halfway with water. Drip in your choice of food coloring—only about two drops per cup.
2. Snap the bottoms off the celery. Place one celery stalk in each cup of colored water. Stir.
3. Draw a line with your marker on the outside of each cup to indicate the water level.
4. Put the cups onto the tray and place the tray on or near a windowsill in the sun. Let it sit there all day and overnight.
5. The next day look at the stalks and leaves. Do you see any new colors? Also check the water level—did it get lower?
6. Snap a piece of your celery in half or peel off the outer layer. Can you see the lines of color?
7. You just saw a celery plant sip water all the way to its leaves! Awesome!

Other ideas to try this experiment with:

☆ A carrot
☆ A leek
☆ A stick or twig
☆ A leaf, sticking only the stem into the water
☆ A white carnation flower with its stem still attached

FUN . . .
You Can Eat

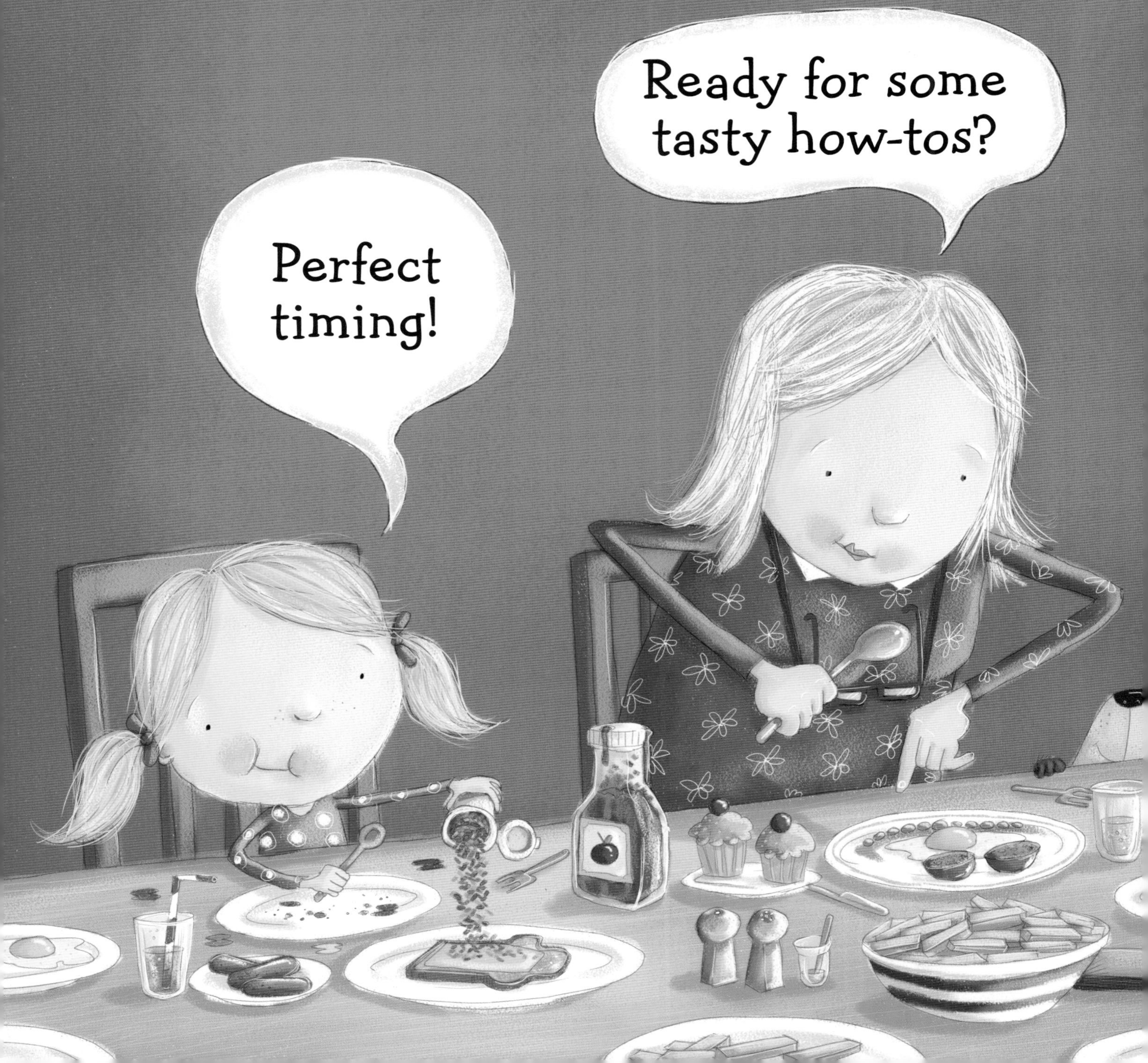

How to Make Raspberry Lemonade

SUPPLIES YOU'LL NEED:

Five large lemons
Two handfuls of
    raspberries
A pitcher
A wooden spoon

2½ cups cold water
¾ cup sugar
Two handfuls of ice
Two cups

STEPS:

1. Wash the lemons and raspberries.
2. Have a grown-up cut the lemons in half. Remove all the seeds. Squeeze the juice into a pitcher or ask a grown-up to use a juicer and then pour the juice into the pitcher.
3. Put the raspberries into the pitcher and use a wooden spoon to smash them right into the lemon juice.
4. Add the cold water. Then add the sugar and stir, stir, stir!
5. Drop in two handfuls of ice and stir some more.
6. Pour two cups of lemonade— one for you and one for your grown-up.
7. Clink your cups and say, "Cheers!"

Other ideas:

☆ Try adding blueberries.
☆ Instead of five lemons, try three lemons and three limes.
☆ Try adding some fresh lavender or basil.

How to Make Breakfast in Bed

SUPPLIES YOU'LL NEED:

Berries
Spoons
Yogurt
Granola
A small plastic cup
Bagel
A plate

A butter knife
Cream cheese or butter
Orange juice
A large plastic cup
A tray
Paper
A marker

STEPS:

1. Make sure Mom or Dad are still asleep and ask another grown-up to help (like Grandma or Grandpa). Tiptoe to the kitchen together. These instructions are for one portion, but make as many as you need!
2. Wash the berries in water.
3. Scoop two spoonfuls of yogurt into a small cup. Drop a handful of berries on top of the yogurt. Repeat yogurt-berries-yogurt-berries until you reach nearly the top of the cup. Sprinkle granola on the very top.
4. Next, have your grown-up cut the bagel and put it on a plate.
5. Open up the bagel and spread cream cheese or butter onto both sides using the knife.
6. Pour orange juice (or whatever kind you have!) into the large cup.
7. Place the food and drink onto a tray and include utensils. Make it all look fancy.
8. Fold a piece of paper in half. Draw a picture and write "I love YOU!"
9. Carefully carry the tray into your parent's room and say, "Surprise! Breakfast in bed!" Hand them the tray and then take a quick bite to make sure everything tastes delicious!

Other ideas for making breakfast in bed:

- ☆ A tortilla spread with cream cheese and jam, rolled up
- ☆ Avocado toast with a slice of cheese and cold hard-boiled egg
- ☆ Instant oatmeal topped with blueberries, cinnamon, and almonds

How to Make a Pizza

SUPPLIES YOU'LL NEED:

A dish towel or apron
Foil or parchment paper
A baking sheet
Pizza crust (pre-made)

A spoon
Pizza sauce
Shredded cheese
Pepperoni or other toppings

STEPS:

1. Run to your dress-up box and find your chef's hat and apron—or use a dish towel as an apron!

2. Ask a grown-up to preheat the oven to 375 degrees Fahrenheit.

3. Pull out a piece of foil or parchment paper and line a baking sheet with it, then put the pizza crust on it.

4. Scoop a few spoonfuls of pizza sauce right onto the middle of the crust. Using the back of the spoon, smear the sauce around until the whole crust is covered except for the very edges.

5. Sprinkle shredded cheese so that the red sauce is covered.

6. Decorate with pepperoni or other toppings, however you please!

7. Ask a grown-up to put the pizza into the oven until the cheese has melted— about 12 to 15 minutes.

8. Have your grown-up slice you a piece and put it on a plate. Sprinkle it with parmesan cheese and oregano, then dig in! Lip-smacking good!

Ideas for topping designs:

⭐ A happy face
⭐ A star
⭐ A tic-tac-toe game
⭐ A heart

How to Make
Ice Cream in a Bag

SUPPLIES YOU'LL NEED:

A sandwich-sized plastic zip bag

Half-and-half

Vanilla extract

Sugar

A gallon-sized plastic zip bag

Ice

Rock salt

Gloves or mittens

Chocolate syrup

Sprinkles

A spoon

STEPS:

1. Open the sandwich-sized zip bag. Pour in one cup of half-and-half, one teaspoon of vanilla extract, and two tablespoons of sugar. Seal the bag tightly and massage it gently to mix. Set it aside. Remember, a tight seal is VERY important.

2. Fill your gallon-sized zip bag with ice until it is two-thirds full. Then dump in half a cup of rock salt. Put on your warm gloves or mittens. Swish around the ice and salt just a little by gently tipping the large bag.

3. Place your tightly closed sandwich bag with the milk mixture into the bag of ice, and then tightly seal the bag of ice.

4. Put on your favorite song, hold the sealed side of the gallon bag in one hand and another part of the bag with another and then shake the bag like crazy while dancing. You may have to shake-dance for two songs to make sure your ice cream freezes. Be careful that the seal remains tightly closed while you shake-dance!

5. Once the half-and-half mixture appears to be solid or firm, pull it out of the ice bag. You can take off your gloves now.

6. Open the ice cream bag and load it up with chocolate syrup and sprinkles.

7. Grab a spoon and dig in. Who knew that dancing could be so sweet!

Ideas for other toppings:

- ☆ Gummy bears
- ☆ Chocolate chips
- ☆ Blueberries and almonds
- ☆ Crushed-up cookies

How to Make Bugs on a Log

SUPPLIES YOU'LL NEED:

Two stalks of celery
A spoon

Peanut butter
Raisins

STEPS:

1. Wash the celery stalks.
2. Snap the celery stalks into finger-length sticks.
3. Use the spoon to smear peanut butter into the middle part of the celery sticks.
4. Place raisins on top.
5. Lick the spoon and then eat your creations!

Other ideas to try:

- ⭐ Carrots with almond butter and chocolate chips
- ⭐ Cucumber with cream cheese and roasted chickpeas
- ⭐ Celery with ricotta cheese and halved cherry tomatoes
- ⭐ Roasted zucchini with hummus and olives

How to Bake
Snickerdoodle Cookies

INGREDIENTS

Cookies

Cookie sheet
Parchment paper (optional)
2 medium bowls
2¾ cups flour
2 teaspoons cream of tartar
2 teaspoons cinnamon
1 teaspoon baking soda
⅛ teaspoon salt
1 cup soft butter
1½ cups white sugar
2 eggs
1 teaspoon vanilla
A spatula or wooden spoon
A cooling rack or plate

Topping

A small bowl
A fork
¼ cup sugar
1 tablespoon cinnamon

STEPS:

1. Ask your grown-up to preheat the oven to 375 degrees Fahrenheit. Cover the bottom of the cookie sheet with parchment paper, if you have it.

2. In a medium bowl, mix the flour, cream of tartar, cinnamon, baking soda, and salt together. Set aside.

3. Put the butter and sugar into another medium bowl. Ask your grown-up to plug in an electric handheld mixer. Beat the sugar and butter together until they are fluffy.

4. Add one egg at a time into the butter and sugar mixture. Mix in the vanilla extract.

5. Using a spatula or wooden spoon, add in the flour mixture a little at a time until it's all mixed in.

6. In a small bowl, using a fork, mix the sugar and cinnamon for the topping.

7. Use the spatula to scoop out spoonfuls of dough and then shape them into balls with your hands. Roll the balls into the topping mixture so they are covered in cinnamon-sugar yumminess.

8. Place the balls two inches apart on your cookie sheet. Have your grown-up put it into the oven. Bake for 9 to 11 minutes.

9. Have your grown-up pull out the cookies and let them cool on the cookie sheet for five minutes.

10. Once cooled, place cookies on two small plates—one for you and one for your grown-up—and serve alongside two cups of milk. Enjoy!

How to Paint a Rock

SUPPLIES YOU'LL NEED:

Smooth, round rocks that are light in color
Old newspaper, parchment paper, or
   construction paper
Tempera paint
Small paper cups or a paper plate
Paintbrushes
Paper towels
Glue
Googly eyes and stickers
Glitter (optional)

STEPS:

1. Head outside with a grown-up to find the rocks. Choose at least five.
2. Lay some paper on the table to catch any mess. Squirt the paint into the cups or plate.
3. Decorate the rocks. If you paint your rock, let it dry before adding stickers or using glue to add googly eyes.
4. Sit back and admire your rock-tastic artwork!

Ideas for using your painted rocks:

☆ Place them along the walkway of your house.
☆ Keep one as a pet rock.
☆ Put a bow on them and give them away as gifts.
☆ If you added googly eyes, use the rocks in a Rock and Roll Puppet Show.

How to Make a
Spiral Friendship Bracelet

Different-colored embroidery floss or string
Kid-safe scissors
Tape

STEPS:

1. Take one string and wrap it loosely around your wrist four times, paying attention to where the string stops. Holding where you want to cut the string, unwind it from your wrist and snip it.

2. Use that cut string to measure out the length for the other pieces. Snip them to the same length. You'll need six strings. They can all be the same color or different colors.

3. Gather your strings and tie a tight knot two inches from one end, so all of the strings are knotted together.

4. Tape down the knotted end to a table so it won't move while you make your bracelet.

5. Start with the strand of your favorite color. Make a loop on top of the other (straight) colors so together they look like the number 4, with your favorite color making a long arm that goes across the other strings.

6. Now, with the long arm still over the strands, take the end of the long arm and weave it back underneath your other strands. Pull that end from underneath up into the fold of the number 4, looping it up and through so it completes a circle around the straight strings.

7. Holding the straight strings with one hand so they don't move, pull the end of the looped piece up toward the knotted end, tightening it so the 4 becomes an oval that shrinks into a small loop, knotting around the tight strands.

8. Continue doing this same thing (make a 4 shape, wrap around and under the straight strands, pull up and through the sharp point of the 4, then tighten) until you are ready to switch to a new color. Remember to pull tightly—none of the other color strands should be showing through.

9. To switch to a different color, just grab a new string, move the color you are done using so it joins the straight strings, and continue with the same 4-shape pattern until you are ready to switch again. (If you are using only one color for all six strands, you'll want to occasionally change which piece is making the knots so you don't run out of one strand.)

10. As you work, you can wrap the bracelet around your wrist to see how long it is by holding your wrist on top of the knot and pulling up the loose strands, but just don't take the tape off until you are done. Once it's as long as you'd like it to be, remove the tape. Put the bracelet around your wrist and ask a friend or grown-up to tie the edges together in a knot. Make sure you've left extra length at the end!

11. Make friendship bracelets for your friends!

How to Make a
Scritchy-Scratch Drawing

Crayons, including several black ones
Paper
A toothpick

1. Color the paper using the non-black crayons. Make designs—abstract art with shapes and squiggles or pictures of anything you choose. Just fill the whole page with color.

2. With your black crayons, color over everything on the page. Yes, everything! Press hard—you want the whole page pitch-black!

3. Use the toothpick point to draw by scraping away the black. Make

squiggles, shapes, designs, letters—anything you like. Can you see the color coming through?

4. Show your scritchy-scratch drawing to your family. They will be amazed!

Ideas of designs to make:

☆ Cover the page with lots of different-colored squares of varying sizes. Then, after coloring black crayon over your colorful squares, use the toothpick to scratch out more different-sized squares.

☆ Color your page with rainbow-colored stripes, starting with a red stripe on the left side, then an orange one, and moving through all the colors of the rainbow (red, orange, yellow, green, blue, indigo, and violet) or all the colors of YOUR rainbow (make up your own pattern!), ending with violet or your own color on the right.

☆ Write out a secret message using different colors on the page, and color around the words of your message. Then color over everything with black crayon. Put your message and a toothpick in an envelope and give it to someone special. Tell them to scratch off the black until the message is revealed.

How to Press a Flower

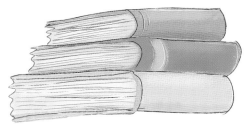

Fresh flowers
Paper towels
Parchment paper
Flat cardboard pieces
Many large books (you may need a grown-up's help with this)

STEPS:

1. Find some beautiful flowers in your garden. Ask a grown-up for permission to pick a few, and take them inside. Or ask a grown-up to go on a walk with you to find some flowers in the wild that you can pick and bring home.

2. Use a paper towel to carefully pat your flowers dry if they are damp. You don't want any dew or water on them.

3. Rip a large square of parchment paper and place the flowers on one half of the paper. Lay the flowers carefully so they are not touching. Only a few flowers may fit on the paper. Fold the remaining half of the parchment paper over the flowers, almost like a book.

4. Slide a piece of cardboard under the parchment paper, and place another piece of cardboard on top.

5. Open one of the large books. Gently lift your cardboard-parchment-flower sandwich and put it on one of the open book pages. Slowly close the book so the pressed flower materials are inside it.

6. Put the book with the flowers in a safe spot, and pile the other heavy books on top.

7. Wait three weeks and then take the heavy books off and open the book with the flowers.

8. Admire your beautiful pressed flowers!

Ideas of what to do with your pressed flowers:

☆ Glue them to a sheet of paper to make an artistic picture or a card.

☆ Glue them to a strip of paper and slide them into a plastic bookmark sleeve.

☆ Place them in a small picture frame.

How to Make
Tape-and-Paint Art

SUPPLIES YOU'LL NEED:

Acrylic paint
A paper plate (or muffin tin, if your grown-up says it's okay)
Painter's tape
Canvas rectangles or thick cardboard boxes opened flat
Paintbrushes

STEPS:

1. Squirt different colors of paint onto a paper plate, or into each spot in the muffin tin. Try not to mix the colors just yet.

2. Rip the painter's tape into different sizes and then press it onto your canvas or flattened cardboard box to make a design. Don't cover the whole thing, just the parts where you want the white (or brown) of the canvas (or cardboard box) to show through. Press the tape down firmly.

3. Once your tape design is in place, paint the canvas. Make any kind of designs you like. And yes, paint over the tape, too.
4. Let the paint dry completely.
5. Carefully peel off the tape. What did your design reveal?

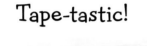

Tape-tastic!

Ideas of what to create with the tape:

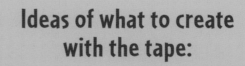

- ☆ Your name spelled out
- ☆ Flowers or stars
- ☆ A spiderweb
- ☆ Trees
- ☆ Hearts
- ☆ A sign for your room

How to Make
Fruit and Veggie Prints

Different fruits and vegetables

Paper towels

A marker

Paint

Small bowls or plates

Paper

66

STEPS:

1. Ask a grown-up to slice your fruits and vegetables in half. Pat the half of each fruit and vegetable you are going to use with a paper towel to clean away any extra juice. Save the other half of each for a snack.

2. If you are using carrots or potatoes, have your grown-up cut them into discs.

3. Use a marker to draw a shape on the discs (such as a star or a heart) and ask the adult to cut away the extra.

4. Squirt different colors of paint into separate bowls or small plates.

5. Dip your fruit or vegetable into the paint and press it down onto your paper. Look at that cool print!

6. Repeat this with different colors and different fruits and vegetables.

Ideas of produce you can use for your prints:

☆ Oranges, lemons, and bell peppers sliced in half

☆ Apples or mushrooms sliced from top to bottom

☆ Broccoli or cauliflower, dipping the bushy part into the paint

☆ Bok choy or leeks, cutting the base off from side to side, and using just the base

☆ The possibilities are endless!

FUN . . .
with Imagin-YAY-tion

How to Make a Costume Parade

SUPPLIES YOU'LL NEED:

Card stock or thin cardboard
  (such as from a cereal box)
Kid-safe scissors
Markers
Glitter glue

Sequins
Popsicle sticks
Dress-up props
Toilet paper rolls or paper
  towel rolls

STEPS:

1. First, make a mask by cutting large ovals out of card stock or cardboard. Cut out the mask's eyes and mouth and then decorate the mask using markers, glitter glue, sequins—whatever you have. Glue a Popsicle stick to the bottom of each mask.

2. Search through your costume chest or toy box for hats, feather boas, gloves—be creative!

3. Color the toilet paper rolls or paper towel rolls. Perfect for horn-blowing.

4. Put on all your costume pieces, hold up your masks, and put your horns up to your mouths.

5. Parade through the house blasting your horns.

How to Make a Treasure Map

Paper
Markers
A special treasure to hide
An envelope or small box
A ribbon or rubber band

STEPS:

1. Head to the backyard with the paper and some markers. Look around and really check out the space.

2. On your paper, draw the yard. If you have a bench back there, draw the bench on your map. Give it a silly name. Continue drawing and naming other items until you have mapped out your whole backyard and labeled everything.

3. Add in some imaginary landmarks, and maybe even some mythical beasts protecting the treasure.

4. Now, decide WHAT your treasure will be. Put the treasure into an envelope or small box. Find a spot in your backyard, dig a hole, hide the treasure inside, and cover the hole back up.

5. Draw a big red X on the map to mark where you hid the treasure.

6. Crumple up your map and make it all wrinkly. Uncrumple it and roll it up. Place a ribbon or a rubber band around it and hand it to your grown-up.

7. Say, "Ahoy, matey, this be a treasure map. X marks the spot!"

8. Watch your grown-up travel the seven seas—of your backyard—to find the treasure. Did they succeed?

Ideas for treasure:

- ✩ A miniature car
- ✩ A friendship bracelet
- ✩ Some raisins
- ✩ A note with a hidden message

How to Create a Shoe Shop

SUPPLIES YOU'LL NEED:

Paper

Markers and crayons

Tape

A chair

A toy cash register or small box

Lots of different shoes

Kid-safe scissors

STEPS:

1. Make a sign that says, "Shoe Shop, Today Only!" Tape it up on the wall or your door. Get a chair and a pretend cash register (a small box works fine for this).

2. Gather up different kinds of shoes. Ask your grown-ups if you can borrow a few of theirs. Arrange the shoes in pairs around the room.

3. Use some paper and markers or crayons to write prices, such as "$22" or "Buy one, get one free."

4. Get some toy money—or make your own using paper, green crayons, and scissors. Add it to your register.

5. In your loudest voice call out, "Shoe store is open for business!"

6. When your first customer comes, give them a tour of the store. Chat them up as you showcase the shoes.

7. Give your customer some of your dollars. Once they make their selection, have them pay for their brand-new shoes.

8. Tell them "Great choice! Thanks for stopping by and please come again."

Find out what shoes your customer needs:

- ⭐ Being fancy? Show them the dress-up shoes.
- ⭐ Going to the pool? Suggest swim fins or flip-flops.
- ⭐ Hiking? Recommend hiking boots.
- ⭐ Sports? Point out the sneakers or cleats.
- ⭐ Lounging? Suggest the bunny slippers.

How to Make a Race Car

Lots and lots of different-sized boxes

Strong, sturdy tape

Paper plates

Art materials to decorate with (paint and paintbrushes, markers, stickers, etc.)

STEPS:

1. Place the largest box on the ground with the flaps open. This will be your driver's seat.

2. Tape some medium-sized boxes to the front of the driver's-seat box.

3. On each side of the driver's-seat box, add some small boxes, taping them tight. These are your pretend side mirrors.

4. Tape some medium-sized boxes along the back, stacking them if you like.

5. For the wheels, tape a medium box on each corner of your car. Then tape a paper plate to each box.

6. Tape a paper plate to the front-inside of your seat box for a steering wheel. Soon you'll be ready to take the wheel!

7. Decorate your race car using paint, markers, stickers, or other art materials. Once the paint is dry, drive into the sunset to a new adventure!

VROOM!

Other ideas of what to build with boxes:

☆ A spaceship
☆ A jet
☆ A submarine
☆ A castle

How to Build a Pirate Cave

SUPPLIES YOU'LL NEED:

A large sheet or blanket
A table
Pillows
A broom
A shirt
Stuffed animals
A large box (optional)

STEPS:

1. Have your grown-up help you drape the sheet or blanket over the table.

2. Gather some pillows—ask permission first! Put the pillows under the hanging sheet and lay them against the legs of the table.

3. Tie a shirt to the top of the broom handle. Lean it against your pirate cave. Pirate flag in place!

4. Bring your stuffed animals as your crew. Show them the pirate cave you've discovered.

5. If you have a large box, place it right beside your cave. That's your getaway boat in case adventure calls!

6. Sing pirate tunes with your grown-up, your first mate, and your whole pirate crew!

How to Make a Sock Puppet Show

SUPPLIES YOU'LL NEED:

Socks that are missing a match

Art supplies (markers, googly eyes, glue, buttons, paint, ribbon, etc.)

A table or couch as a stage

STEPS:

1. Use your art supplies to decorate the socks. Add a face to your puppet: Silly? Scary? Your choice!
2. Create enough sock puppets so everyone can have one, including you! Set them aside to dry if you used glue or paint.

3. Find a table or couch to be the stage. You should be able to safely fit behind it. Or find a large box and decorate it as your stage.

4. Once the socks are dry, have your family members sit in front of the stage.

5. Get behind the stage and put your sock onto your hand. With your best sock puppet voice, introduce the show. Give everyone the puppet you made for them.

6. Take turns being onstage and in the audience. Make a Sock Puppet Show: scary stories, silly stories, and true family stories. Enjoy!

Ideas for the show:

- ✩ Goldilocks and the Three Bears
- ✩ The Three Little Pigs
- ✩ The Hokey Pokey
- ✩ The Itsy Bitsy Spider
- ✩ A puppet talent show

Are those my socks?

How to Play the Subject Jumble Hand Game

STEPS:

1. Sit in a circle with your family. Decide who gets to pick the first subject category.

2. Now, show everyone the rhythm of the game: slap your legs with both hands, clap your hands, then snap your fingers twice. Repeat this cool beat over and over again while chanting: "Sub-ject Jum-ble. Sub-ject Jum-ble. Subject Jumble is the task. Answer while the rhythm lasts."

3. While the rhythm is going, the person who picks the category will say, on beat, "Subject is . . . ," and will then fill in the blank with the category, as well as a name of something that fits into that category. For example, "Subject is Animal. Pig."

4. The person sitting to the right goes next, keeping the rhythm and naming something that fits the category. Continue to move around the circle while everyone keeps the rhythm, each person in turn calling out something that fits the category.

5. If someone can't think of something in time (four beats is all they get) or they miss the rhythm, they are out and the category switches. Also, you can't repeat a word once it's mentioned or you are out.

Ideas for categories:

☆ Animals
☆ Types of cars
☆ Fruits and vegetables
☆ States in the United States
☆ Favorite books

How to Play Picture Guess with Someone Far Away

SUPPLIES YOU'LL NEED:

Paper or a whiteboard
A pen or dry erase marker
A cup
Kid-safe scissors (optional)
A timer

STEPS:

1. Make a video call to Grandma or Grandpa or another adult. Ask them if they want to play a game. When they say yes, tell them to get either paper and a pen, or a whiteboard and dry erase markers. You'll need these, too.

2. On a separate piece of paper, both of you write down at least ten different things you will draw. Keep them hidden. Then cut out or tear apart the words and put them into a cup.

3. Decide who goes first. They pull out a word from their cup.

4. Set the timer for three minutes. Holding up the whiteboard or paper so it can be seen on-screen, the person draws a picture to match the word, while the guesser tries to guess it.

5. If the guesser gets it right before the time runs out, they get a point. If the guesser runs out of time, no one gets a point.

6. Now switch roles.

7. Continue until all the words are used.

8. Play, laugh, and have a blast!

Ideas of things to draw:

☆ A camel
☆ An apple
☆ An airplane
☆ A house

How to Throw a Surprise Party

SUPPLIES YOU'LL NEED:

Construction paper
Kid-safe scissors
A glue stick
A long piece of paper
Markers
Tape
String or yarn
Good music
Food

STEPS:

1. Have Dad take your sibling on a long outing. Then quick—set up for the surprise party while Mom or another grown-up gets all the tasty food ready.

2. Cut colored construction paper into long strips, one or two inches wide. Glue the two ends of a strip together to make a ring. Loop another strip through your ring and then glue the two ends together so you now have two interconnected loops. Continue until you've made a long, colorful chain. Hang it up.

3. On a long piece of paper, write the words "We love you!" and "Surprise!" Hang it up near the door.

4. Make a party hat! Decorate a sheet of paper with lots of colors. Roll the sheet to form a cone, and tape the edge. Cut two lengths of string or yarn and tape them to the bottom edge of the cone. Repeat this to make hats for the whole family or your friends!

5. Find your sibling's favorite music and have it ready to go. Don't turn it on yet.

6. When Dad pulls up with your sibling, turn off the lights. Everyone hide.

7. When the door opens, jump out, switch on the lights, and shout, "SURPRISE!!!"

8. Turn on the music and let the party begin!

Things to do at the party:

⭐ Sing karaoke
⭐ Play freeze dance
⭐ Do a family line dance all together
⭐ Play twenty-one questions

How to Make It Rain in Your House

STEPS:

1. Gather all your family members. Tell them you can make it rain in the house, with their help. No need for an umbrella!
2. Have everyone sit in a circle and copy exactly what you do. Tell them to listen only and follow your lead but not to say anything!
3. First, snap your fingers on each hand very slowly, one after the other. Have your family copy you. Snap faster and faster and faster. Can you hear the rain picking up?
4. Now, rub your hands together over and over again, really fast. Listen closely.
5. Next, pat your legs quickly over and over again.
6. Finally, begin stomping your feet over and over again. Oh no! It's a downpour!
7. What's that, the storm is starting to calm again? Go back to patting your legs over and over again, getting slower and slower. Then move back to rubbing your hands, slowing down some more.
8. Last, go back to snapping your fingers, one hand then the other, slowing completely down. Then stop.
9. Congratulations—you just created a storm in your very own home! Try it again but with your eyes closed!

How to Teach Mom Yoga

SUPPLIES YOU'LL NEED:

A yoga mat, blanket, or towel
Reusable water bottles

STEPS:

1. Stretch your body to get ready. Fill the water bottles. Find a soft, open place on the ground outside or in your home. Ask your mom if she's ready.

2. First, show her how to stand up straight with both feet on the ground. Have her breathe in and out deeply. She should raise one foot off the ground by bending her knee and balancing on her other foot. Then have her put her hands in front of her chest like she is praying. Breathe. She is now in the Tree Pose.

3. Next, she should put her hands and knees on the ground like a dog. Tell her to spread her fingers wide. Have her raise her hips so her bottom is in the air and her toes and hands are still on the ground. She's doing a Downward-Facing Dog Pose. Breathe.

4. Then have her slowly drop her bottom so that her hips and legs are now flat on the ground and her arms are still straight, palms down. Her chest and face should be up. Now she's doing the Cobra Pose. Breathe deeply.

5. Tell your adult to sit on her bottom and cross her legs, crisscross applesauce. Have her place her hands together in front of her chest like she's praying. Hold your hands together, too, bow, and tell her she did an amazing job! Take a sip of water!

How to WOW
with a Magic Show

SUPPLIES YOU'LL NEED:

A magician's hat and cape (a blanket will work fine)
A pencil
Three quarters
Aluminum foil
Kid-safe scissors

STEPS:

1. Search your toybox for a magician's hat and a magician's cape (blankets work well, too). Put on your hat and cape.
2. Prepare your tricks first by taking a small piece of foil and putting it on top of one of your quarters. Press down hard on the foil and rub your finger across it so that it creates the indentations of the quarter. Once you are finished, the piece of foil should have a mold of the quarter.
3. Cut the quarter mold out so it looks like a shiny new quarter, and set it aside carefully so it does not crease. Be sure it is hidden, though, so your audience can't see it.
4. Find your family members and say, "Here ye! Here ye! Come to the living room for my magic show!"

5. Once everyone is seated, say that you are a magician and you will perform some amazing magic tricks.

6. Trick one: Tell them your pencil is just an ordinary pencil and shake it in front of them. Then say, "Or is it . . ."

7. Now, hold the pencil loosely between your index finger and thumb. Quickly, move your hand up and down to shake the pencil so it looks as if it is bending in the middle—you may need to practice this a few times before your big show! Shout out: "MAGIC! Now watch this!"

8. Trick two: Hold the pencil like a wand and tell them that it is not a pencil at all, but a magic wand! Place the three quarters and the fake foil quarter in your palm, with the foil one blocked a bit by the real quarters. Count aloud to four, then say, "I will make one quarter disappear!"

9. Put the other quarters down on a table or the floor, all except your foil one. Wave the magic pencil wand and say your magic words. Then quickly close your hand, crushing the foil. Wave your hands, carefully dropping the foil ball so others can't see, then open your hand, revealing that the quarter has disappeared.

10. Bow to your clapping fans and thank them for attending your magic show.

How to Play Twenty-One Questions over Video

SUPPLIES YOU'LL NEED:

A sheet of paper
A pen
Kid-safe scissors (optional)
A cup

STEPS:

1. Sit back and think about all the fun things you've done with Grandma or Grandpa. Look at family photos to jog your memory.

2. What questions do you want to ask them? On a sheet of paper, make a column of numbers from 1 to 21—you can turn it over to finish on the back. Write (or draw) your first question next to the number 1.

3. Repeat until you have twenty-one questions. Add more paper if needed.

4. Now take another piece of paper and write the numbers 1 to 21. Cut out or tear apart each number and put them in a cup.

5. Get help video-calling Grandma and Grandpa. Once they come on, ask if they want to play a question game.

6. Tell them you wrote twenty-one questions and that you will take turns asking and answering them.

7. Pick a number from your cup. Ask the question that matches the number you picked. Let your grandparents answer, then you answer.

8. Continue until you've asked all the questions.

9. Have a blast getting to know your grandparents even better.

Ideas of questions to ask:

✫ What happened on the best day of your life?

✫ What is your favorite dessert?

✫ If you had three wishes, what would you wish for?

✫ If you could visit one place you've never been, where would you go?

✫ If you had one million dollars, what would you spend it on?

✫ Who taught you to swim?

✫ Who fixed breakfast when you were growing up and what did you eat?

✫ What was your favorite book (or comic book) when you were little?

How to Make a Family Memory

SUPPLIES YOU'LL NEED:

Snacks

Water

Tote bag

Frisbee

Football

Jump ropes

A bouncy ball

Two cloths or bandannas

STEPS:

1. Invite your family to the park.
2. Pack a tote bag with snacks and water, and some exciting games like a Frisbee, a football, jump ropes, a bouncy ball, and two cloths or bandannas (for playing capture the flag).
3. As your family arrives, get them to agree: no electronic devices. Put all phones and other devices in a bag. *All* of them. Seal the bag tightly.
4. Open up the tote bag and, as a family, decide what you are going to do first.
5. Once you've all decided, play, play, PLAY! Take a quick snack break and then continue playing together until it's time to go.
6. Hand everyone their devices back. Snap a family picture.
7. Hug your family, tell them how much you love them, and say, "We've *got* to do this again."

Checklist

- ☐ How to Make an Easy-Peasy Kite
- ☐ How to Plant a Seed
- ☐ How to Make a Leaf Collector's Book
- ☐ How to Camp in Your Backyard
- ☐ How to Make a Snowman
- ☐ How to Enjoy a Picnic
- ☐ How to Go Stargazing
- ☐ How to Make a Mosaic
- ☐ How to Make a Snowflake
- ☐ How to Send a Letter to Grandpa
- ☐ How to Make Your Own Book
- ☐ How to Make Your Own Puzzle
- ☐ How to Make and Play Animal Card Memory
- ☐ How to Make Super-Spy Ink
- ☐ How to Build a Volcano
- ☐ How to Make a Lava Lamp
- ☐ How to Make Goop
- ☐ How to Watch a Vegetable Drink
- ☐ How to Make Raspberry Lemonade
- ☐ How to Make Breakfast in Bed
- ☐ How to Make a Pizza
- ☐ How to Make Ice Cream in a Bag
- ☐ How to Make Bugs on a Log
- ☐ How to Bake Snickerdoodle Cookies

- ☐ How to Paint a Rock
- ☐ How to Make a Spiral Friendship Bracelet
- ☐ How to Make a Scritchy-Scratch Drawing
- ☐ How to Press a Flower
- ☐ How to Make Tape-and-Paint Art
- ☐ How to Make Fruit and Veggie Prints
- ☐ How to Make a Costume Parade
- ☐ How to Make a Treasure Map
- ☐ How to Create a Shoe Shop
- ☐ How to Make a Race Car
- ☐ How to Build a Pirate Cave
- ☐ How to Make a Sock Puppet Show
- ☐ How to Play the Subject Jumble Hand Game
- ☐ How to Play Picture Guess with Someone Far Away
- ☐ How to Throw a Surprise Party
- ☐ How to Make It Rain in Your House
- ☐ How to Teach Mom Yoga
- ☐ How to WOW with a Magic Show
- ☐ How to Play Twenty-One Questions over Video
- ☐ How to Make a Family Memory